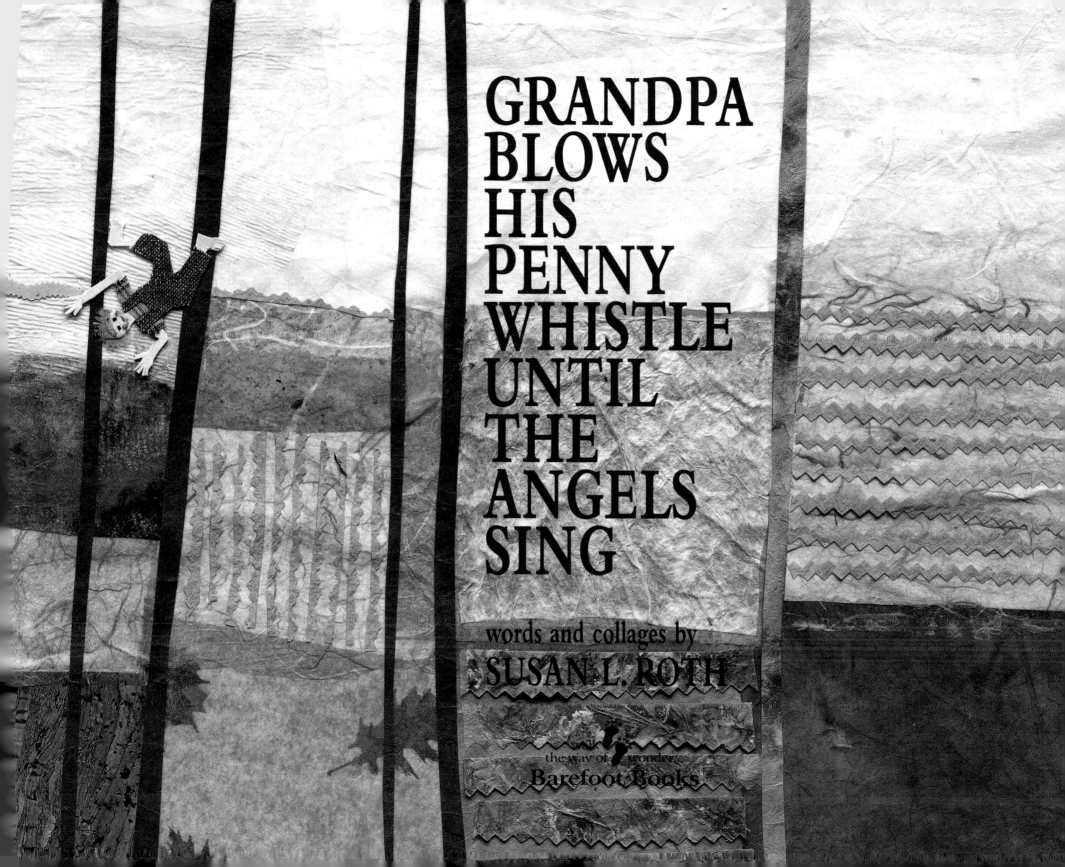

GRANDPA BLOWS HIS PENNY WHISTLE UNTIL THE ANGELS SING

words and collages by

SUSAN L. ROTH

the way of wonder

Barefoot Books

Artist's Note

The colors of this book come from my childhood memories of late summer in heartland America: heat; bleached-out fields; long, low sun; dusty, dry days.

My choice of papers is independent of this, and as illogical as ever. Most of the papers come from Oregon Art Supply in Eugene; a few from some places in Queens, including Sleppin's Dollhouses and Miniatures; and everything else from my endless bounty collected from all over the rest of the world.

Susan L. Roth

Barefoot Books
37 West 17th Street
4th Floor East
New York, New York 10011

This book is printed on 100% acid-free paper

Graphic design by Jennie Hoare, England
Typeset in 18pt Bembo Bold
Color separation by Color Gallery, Malaysia
Printed and bound in Hong Kong by South China Printing Co. (1988) Ltd.

1 3 5 7 9 8 6 4 2

Acknowledgments
I wish to thank Joan Carris, Ann Finnell, Susan Hepler, Nancy Patz, Shirley Rogers-Newman, Diane Rose, Alana Roth, Alex Roth, Alisa Roth.

I wish especially to thank Jesse Roth and Tessa Strickland for their visions and for their faiths.

And I also wish to thank, with appreciation and with love, Ryann Swan Morris.

U.S. Cataloging-in-Publication Data
(Library of Congress Standards)

Roth, Susan L.
Grandpa blows his penny whistle until the angels sing / written and illustrated by Susan L. Roth.—1st ed.
[40]p. : col. ill. ; cm.
Summary: Family love, faith, and singing angels led by Grandpa playing his penny whistle all come together to help rambunctious Little Boy James to recover from his accident.
ISBN 1-84148-247-1
1. Family relationships -- Fiction. 2. Faith -- Fiction. 3. Grandfathers -- Fiction. I. Title.
[E] 21 2001 AC CIP

With appreciation for clergy
who have given me inspiration
even during sermons on hot
summer days:
The Reverend Mr. Max Gaebler
Sister Anne Dyer, RSCJ
Rabbi Dr. Israel Schorr

"I'm not going," says Little Boy James. "Grandpa never goes and I'm not going either."

I smooth down the cool soft pinkness of my Sunday dress.

"Mama'll make you go," I yell, but he doesn't hear because he's already out the door and halfway to the barn.

There's a roar past the window. It sounds like Black Thunder, and it is — our horse, with Little Boy James on top. He's riding bareback even though Mama always tells him not to.

"What's that horse...," she starts, then she's screaming for Papa.

"James, so help me, I can't control that boy. He's out there riding Black Thunder and I've just told him to wash and dress. We'll be late for church."

But Little Boy James is out on the other side of the barn and he can't hear a thing.

"He is incorrigible. Adorable, but incorrigible." Papa goes out onto the porch with his suspenders hanging. "Little Boy!" he shouts.

Grandpa's been playing his penny whistle like always, but now he pulls it out of his mouth. "Leave him be, Elsa," he wheezes from the kitchen rocker. "Look at all that energy. How do you expect him to sit still while the Very Reverend Wilson goes on and on like he does?"

"Papa, please. The Very Reverend is a good man and you know it. He means well even if he does go on and on. That's just his way of talking to God Almighty."

I look out of the
window past Grandpa
and see Black Thunder
walking empty toward
the barn. "He's off the
horse, Mama."

Mama looks out
and there's Little Boy
balancing barefoot on
top of the corral fence
like a tightrope walker.

"I don't care what Grandpa says. When you're as old as Grandpa, you may stay home sometimes, but when you're seven and living in this house, you're going to church with the family."

"That boy!" fumes Mama, and she's out of the door after him. "Get down, Little Boy, or you'll fall and hurt yourself."

"I'm not going, Mama. Grandpa says the Very Reverend Wilson's an old windbag, and I hate the pinchy shoes."

"Mama," he yells. "My shirt collar's scratchy. I'm hot. That old Very Reverend goes on and on and on while the sun is out and the berries need picking."

Little Boy James jumps from the fence and lands like a cat but before Mama can take off toward him, he's away in another direction. There he goes inside the barn, up into the hayloft.

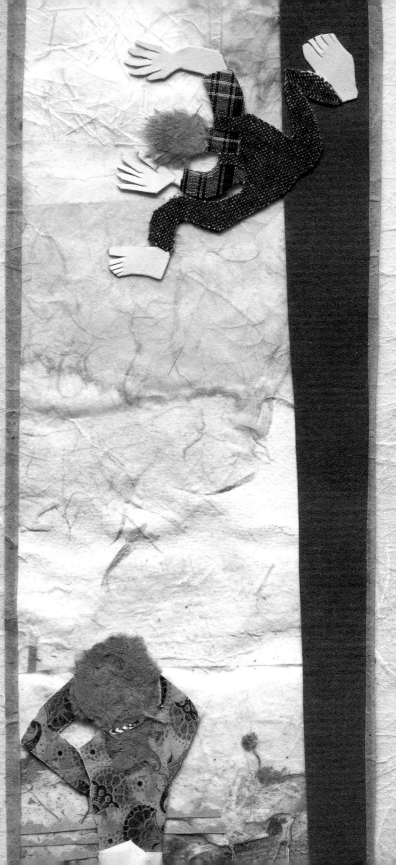

"Little Boy James, I'm getting mad now." Mama wipes her face on her apron, then her hands sit on her hips. "I'm getting all steamed up. Come down right now."

Little Boy jumps and Mama covers her mouth. "You'll break a leg, Little Boy! Get over here right now."

But Little Boy James is out the door and around the side and he's pulling a ladder over to the barn and he's halfway up before Mama even figures which way he's dashing.

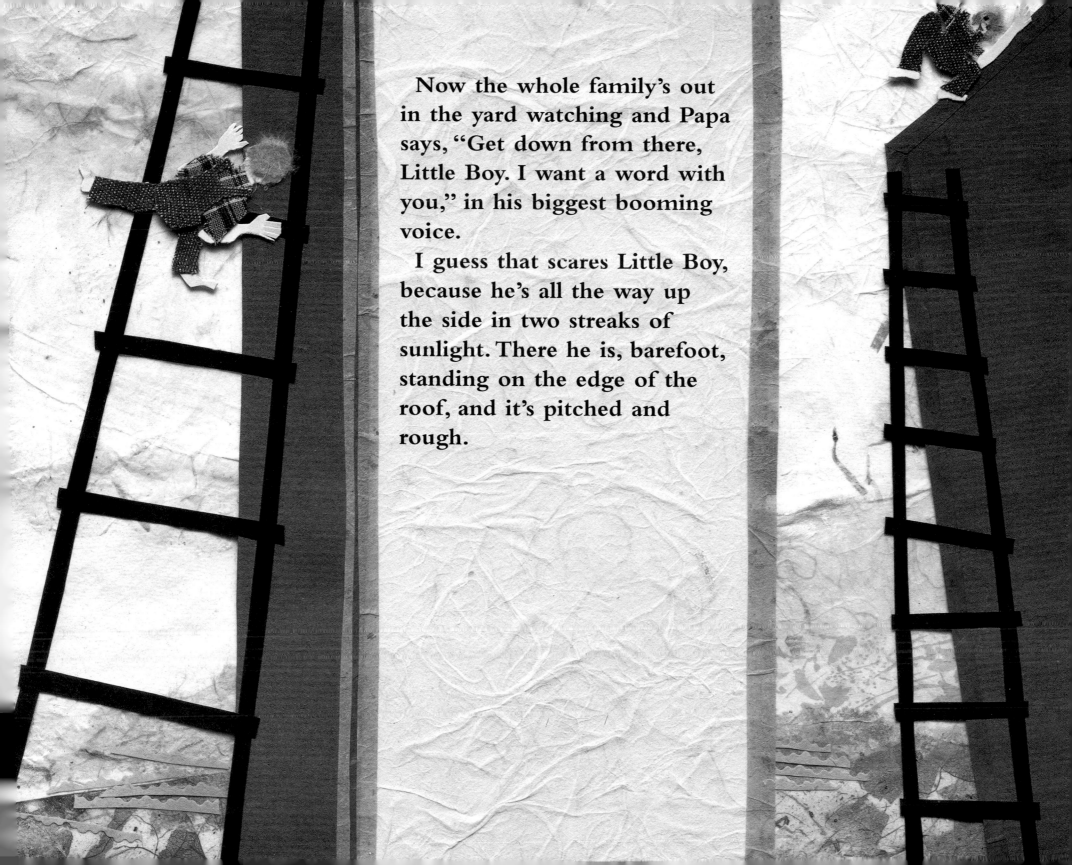

Now the whole family's out in the yard watching and Papa says, "Get down from there, Little Boy. I want a word with you," in his biggest booming voice.

I guess that scares Little Boy, because he's all the way up the side in two streaks of sunlight. There he is, barefoot, standing on the edge of the roof, and it's pitched and rough.

"Aw, Grandpa, I can see all the way to church from up here. There's that stuffy old Very Reverend Wilson in his preacher robe. I'm not going to church, Grandpa. And I guess God Almighty wouldn't go either if He had to listen to the Very Reverend Wilson huffing and spluttering." Little Boy James looks up at the sky, just like he really sees God Almighty. He lifts his arms and he starts to talk.

Grandpa points at Little Boy with his penny whistle. He speaks to him.

"Little Boy Jimmy," says Grandpa, "you may have gone one river too far this time. I'm too old to watch you up there. Now come on down while I hold the ladder for you."

"How did the Very Reverend Wilson get into our church anyway? You should've kicked him out right after the first sermon!"

I'm thinking Little Boy could be sent straight to hell for talking like this.

"Shush your mouth," says Mama, but her mouth shows a third of a smile.

Little Boy is getting all carried away with himself. He seems to think he's right there at the pearly gates, he's up so high anyway, on the edge of the roof, and he acts like he's just getting started.

"You know what? If I were God Almighty, I'd have never let him preach for me. And even if I'm not, I'll never let him preach for me again."

And Little Boy James folds his arms and stamps his foot. He forgets all about being up on the roof of the barn and his foot comes down hard on the ladder, which flips even though Grandpa's holding it, and Little Boy James flies out over the garden. He lands all spread out on his back like he's making an angel in the snow, only he's not moving his wings.

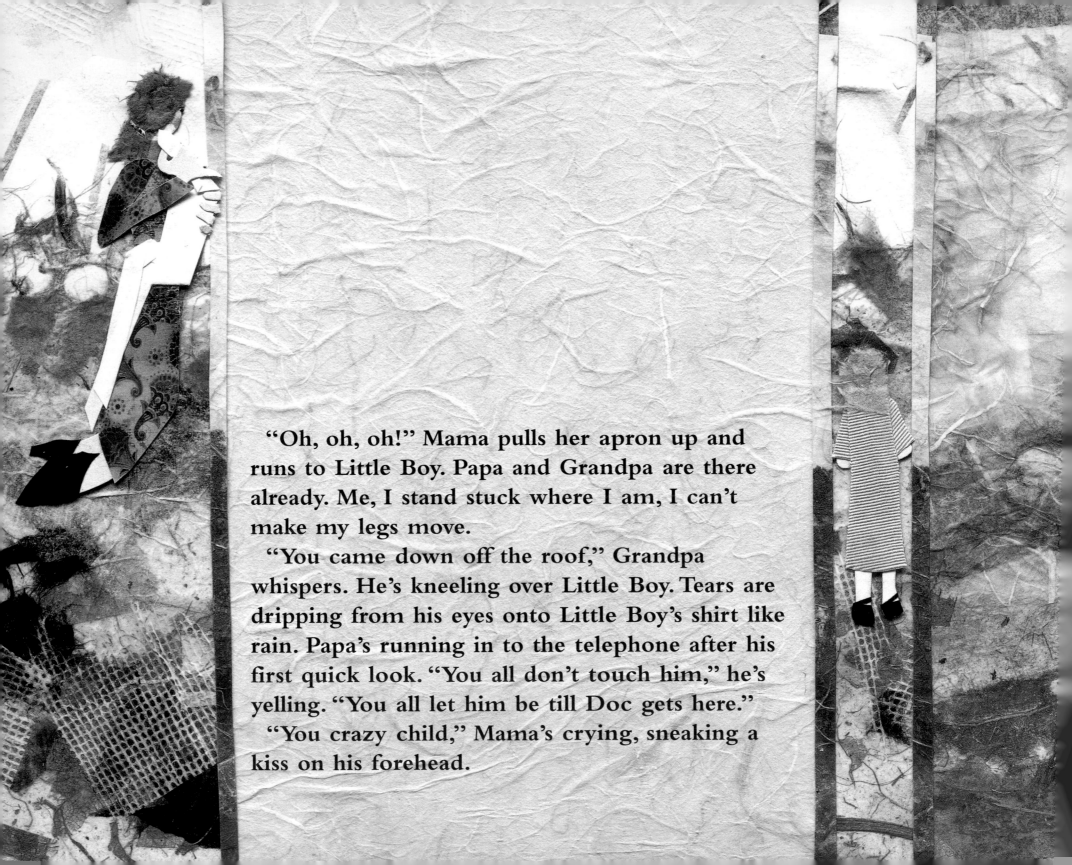

"Oh, oh, oh!" Mama pulls her apron up and runs to Little Boy. Papa and Grandpa are there already. Me, I stand stuck where I am, I can't make my legs move.

"You came down off the roof," Grandpa whispers. He's kneeling over Little Boy. Tears are dripping from his eyes onto Little Boy's shirt like rain. Papa's running in to the telephone after his first quick look. "You all don't touch him," he's yelling. "You all let him be till Doc gets here."

"You crazy child," Mama's crying, sneaking a kiss on his forehead.

"He's dead, he's dead!" Finally, words come from the back of my throat, but it doesn't sound like me talking. I still can't move my legs. "No, Honey, don't worry," Grandpa says in a soft voice. "He's just knocked out." I see he's holding Mama very tight so she can't touch Little Boy James.

It seems like two months till Doc comes driving up, his stethoscope already around his neck. He kneels down on the ground in his Sunday suit, bending over Little Boy, looking in his eyeballs, listening and listening to his little thin chest.

"He's knocked out, Elsa. He's not dead. But who knows what's broken. Little Boy James, speak to me," Doc says. But Little Boy James just lies there.

They make a stretcher out of a sheet. Doc does most of the moving. Very slowly, they bring Little Boy into Mama and Papa's room and lay him on top of the bedspread. He's got a cut on his head which is bleeding a little, but mostly he looks calm and peaceful and still — so unnatural for Little Boy that it's double scary to see him like that.

"Come on, Little Boy," says Doc. "Wake up and talk to us." He dabs at Little Boy's forehead with a cold, wet towel. "No more of this possum stuff. Open your eyes." But Little Boy James stays still and quiet, the first time in his whole life, I think.

Papa's sitting on the chair next to the bed. I can't see his face. "Why didn't I stop him, Elsa, why didn't I stop him sooner?" he says again and again. Mama's kneeling next to Papa and Little Boy; her apron's wringing wet.

"Little Boy," she whispers. "Little Boy, please talk to your Mama and Papa."

My legs are thawed but now I'm just too scared to go close. I stand in the doorway peeking at him lying so still, peeking through my fingers, covering my chicken eyes.

Grandpa's bending over Little Boy
on the other side when Doc looks
up from his stethoscope again.
"We'd better pray a little," Doc says.
"Little Boy's not cooperating."
"He never does," says Mama, with
a shred of her third of a smile.

Grandpa straightens up. His face looks like a broken old cup full of cracks. He turns around and walks sharply out of the room. I see him start from the house and I slip away after him.

"Where are you going, Grandpa?" My hand finds his big hand. "Are you going to get the preacher?"

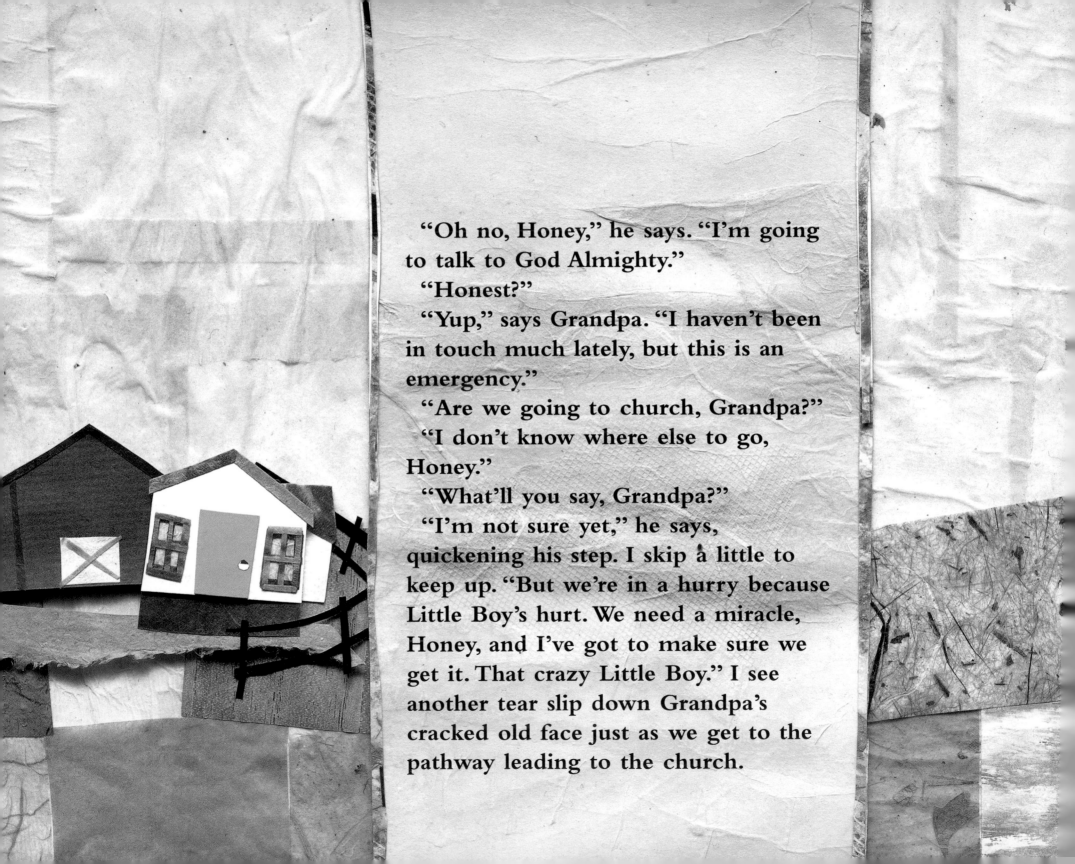

"Oh no, Honey," he says. "I'm going to talk to God Almighty."

"Honest?"

"Yup," says Grandpa. "I haven't been in touch much lately, but this is an emergency."

"Are we going to church, Grandpa?"

"I don't know where else to go, Honey."

"What'll you say, Grandpa?"

"I'm not sure yet," he says, quickening his step. I skip a little to keep up. "But we're in a hurry because Little Boy's hurt. We need a miracle, Honey, and I've got to make sure we get it. That crazy Little Boy." I see another tear slip down Grandpa's cracked old face just as we get to the pathway leading to the church.

The Very Reverend Wilson's vibrating voice is coming out from under the doors, warning us about burning in hell.

"Grandpa, do you think Little Boy's going to hell?"

"No, Honey. That's why I have to talk to God Almighty. Little Boy is much too young, even for heaven."

We walk in through the doors, into the back of the church. I look up at the stained glass window. The sun is shining through in colored ribbons and stripes.

"He's here, all right,"
I whisper. "Mama always
says those light ribbons
are God's countenance
shining down upon us
through the window."

I wait for Grandpa to
speak, but he doesn't say
anything. As the Very
Reverend Wilson drones,
Grandpa moves his
hands like he's talking to
someone, but he still
doesn't say anything. His
face moves, but no words
come out.

Then I see his hand go
into his pocket and get
out his penny whistle.
He carries it up to his
mouth just as natural as
ever and out comes the
loneliest, saddest tune
you ever heard.

The Very Reverend Wilson stops talking right in the middle of his sentence, and all the people turn around in their pews just like when there's a wedding and the bride's about to march in.

Grandpa doesn't even notice, he just blows his penny whistle, the tears falling out of both eyes, his head pointed up to the window. He's talking to God Almighty with the best words he has and everyone in church knows God Almighty is listening. Even the Very Reverend Wilson knows it.

The tears are falling out of my eyes, too, when I see an angel slip through the window: it's a golden angel with a glowing halo, a long, flowing gown and big flying wings.

I rub my eyes to get a better look, and a second angel slips through. Grandpa doesn't notice. He just plays and plays, he doesn't even take a breath.

More and more angels come into the church. They're in rows now, just like the choir on Easter Sunday morning. They fly in on their angel wings, and their angel voices sing Grandpa's sad, crying melody.

The church people are listening in on Grandpa's talk with God Almighty. They stand up in awe, except for the Very Reverend Wilson, who's on his knees.

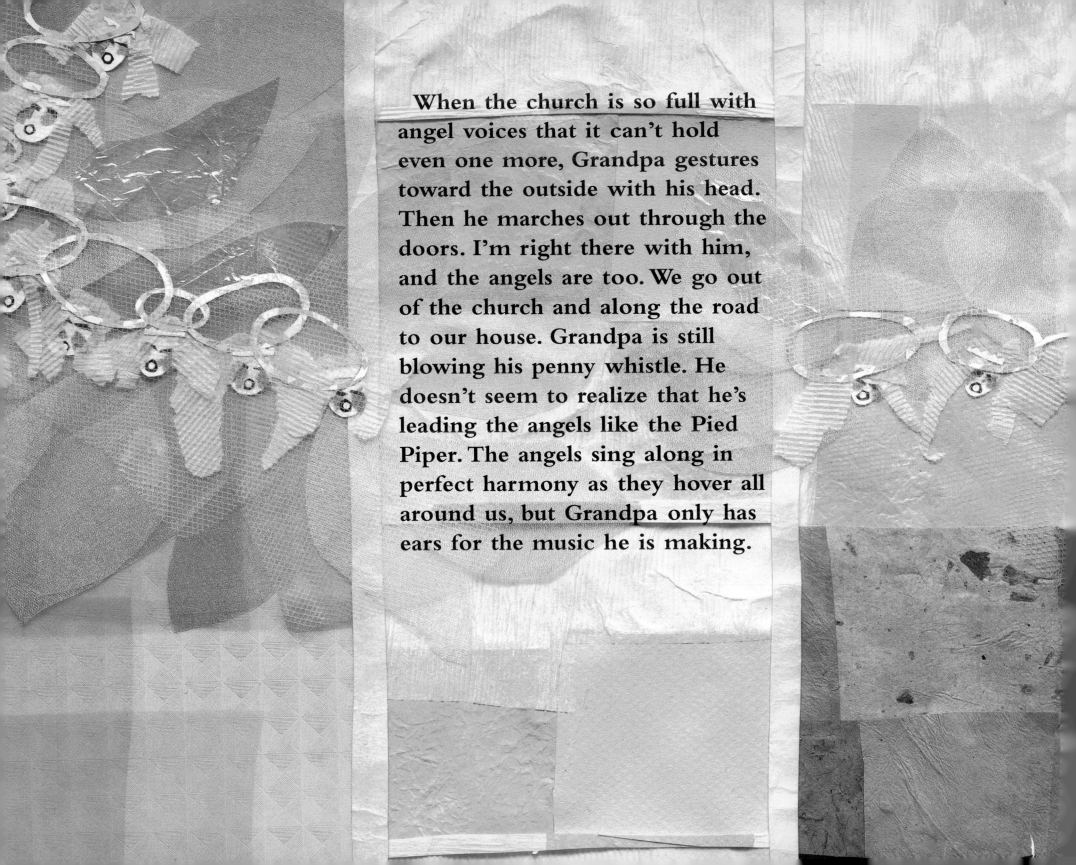

When the church is so full with angel voices that it can't hold even one more, Grandpa gestures toward the outside with his head. Then he marches out through the doors. I'm right there with him, and the angels are too. We go out of the church and along the road to our house. Grandpa is still blowing his penny whistle. He doesn't seem to realize that he's leading the angels like the Pied Piper. The angels sing along in perfect harmony as they hover all around us, but Grandpa only has ears for the music he is making.

We cross our yard, go up the steps, go onto the porch, and I hold the door open for the angels, although they could probably fly right through, even if it were closed.

Grandpa still pays them no mind. He acts as if they don't exist. Blowing his penny whistle, he walks into the bedroom where Little Boy James is lying, still as still as he never is. Grandpa blows a little louder. The angels crowd into the bedroom. Doc, Mama, and Papa don't even look up. They never take their eyes away from Little Boy's face. Grandpa keeps playing his lonely, sad song. The choir of angels sings and sings and sings.

Then Little Boy James
opens his eyes. He sits
up straight and looks
at me.

"When Grandpa blows
his penny whistle," he
says, "I can hear the
angels sing."

Barefoot Books

The barefoot child symbolizes the human being
who is in harmony with the natural world and moves
freely across boundaries of many kinds. Barefoot Books
explores this image with a range of high-quality picture
books for children of all ages. We work with artists,
writers, and storytellers from many cultures, focusing on
themes that encourage independence of spirit, promote
understanding and acceptance of different traditions,
and foster a life long love of learning.

www.barefoot-books.com